Betsy and the Boys

BOOKS BY CAROLYN HAYWOOD

"B" Is for Betsy
Betsy and Billy
Back to School with Betsy
Betsy and the Boys

Here's a Penny
Penny and Peter
Primrose Day
Two and Two Are Four

Betsy and the Boys

Carolyn Haywood

Illustrated by the author

AN ODYSSEY/HARCOURT YOUNG CLASSIC

HARCOURT, INC.

Orlando   Austin   New York   San Diego   Toronto   London

www.HarcourtBooks.com

First Harcourt Young Classics edition 2004
First Odyssey Classics edition 1990
First published 1945

Library of Congress Cataloging-in-Publication Data
Haywood, Carolyn, 1898–
Betsy and the boys/Carolyn Haywood.
p.   cm.
"An Odyssey/Harcourt Young Classic."
Sequel to: Back to school with Betsy.
Summary: Betsy and her fourth-grade friends discover football.
[1. Schools—Fiction.   2. Football—Fiction.]   I. Title.
PZ7.H31496Bg   2004
[Fic]—dc22   2003056555
ISBN 0-15-205106-6   ISBN 0-15-205102-3 (pb)

Printed in the United States of America

A C E G H F D B
A C E G H F D B (pb)

To
Elfrieda Klauder Parker

CONTENTS

Betsy and the Boys

1

Pancakes and Cream Puffs

B etsy, Billy, and Ellen had met in the first grade. They had become fast friends as they worked and played together. For three summers Ellen had gone with Betsy to spend the whole summer on Betsy's grandfather's farm. The third summer Billy had gone too, and the three children had played together for two long months. Now it was September and they were back in their homes, getting ready to return to school.

One morning, the week before school opened, Betsy went over to Billy's house to spend the day. Betsy's mother and Billy's mother were going to a luncheon, so the two children were going to get their own lunch. They were both thrilled, for they loved to cook.

"What are we going to cook?" asked Betsy, as soon as she arrived.

"Pancakes!" shouted Billy. "Pancakes!"

"Oh, yummy!" said Betsy. "They're practically my favorite food, 'cept cream puffs."

Billy's mother came downstairs with her hat and gloves on. "Now, Billy," she said, "don't bother Daddy unless it is absolutely necessary. He's painting a magazine cover and he has to get it finished. I've given him his lunch on a tray."

"O.K.," said Billy.

"And I expect the kitchen to be just as clean when I come back as it is now," said Mrs. Porter. "Don't get the place in a mess."

"Sure, sure," said Billy. "Everything will be dandy. We've cooked at school. We're good."

Billy and Betsy went into the kitchen. Mrs. Porter had left the pancake batter in a pitcher.

The griddle was on the stove.

"I like to make 'em one at a time," said Billy. "That way you can make 'em big."

"I do too," said Betsy.

"I'll make the first one," said Billy. "You get the maple syrup out of the pantry closet."

Betsy went into the pantry. She found the bottle of maple syrup and poured it into a pitcher.

Meanwhile Billy picked up the pitcher of pancake batter to pour it on the griddle. He grasped the pitcher by its handle, but midway between the table and the stove the handle parted from the pitcher and the pitcher fell to the floor, pouring the batter all over the linoleum.

"Hey, Betsy!" Billy yelled. "Come quick!"

Betsy rushed through the pantry door. And then, to Billy's amazement, she slid all the way across the kitchen and right out the back door. There she landed in a heap.

Billy ran toward Betsy, but he too slipped in the batter, which Betsy, as she slid, had spread all over the floor. Billy's slide was exactly like a baseball player sliding to second base.

Miss Mopsie-Upsie Tail, Billy's dog, hearing the racket in the kitchen, came dashing through the pantry door. Like Betsy, she headed straight for the pancake batter. She reached it in a flash. Her legs slid from under her and she skidded on her fat little stomach right out of the door, and joined the children.

Betsy and Billy were so surprised to find themselves in this jumbled mess that for a moment they were speechless. Miss Mopsie-Upsie Tail was the first one on her feet, and before Betsy or Billy had uttered a word she had begun to lick up the pancake batter.

Billy was the first to speak. "Golly! Betsy! Did you hurt yourself?"

"I don't think so," said Betsy.

And then Billy began to laugh. "Gee, but you looked funny sliding out the door."

"Well, you looked funny, too," laughed Betsy. The two children sat on the driveway and rocked with laughter.

Finally they got up. When they looked at each other, they went off into peals again. Betsy's arms and legs were covered with pancake batter. One side of her dress was thick with the white mixture.

"You certainly are a mess," said Billy.

"Well, you don't look so good yourself," laughed Betsy. "You should see the seat of your trousers. You've got about a dozen pancakes right there."

"Maybe I ought to sit on the griddle and bake them," chuckled Billy.

This sent the children off again into fits of laughing.

When they recovered, Billy said, "Well, no kidding. We've lost our lunch."

Betsy did the best she could to wipe the batter off herself with a wet rag.

"If I can find the recipe in the cookbook," said Billy, "I guess we could mix up some more batter."

Billy opened the cookbook. He thumbed through the pages. "Oh, boy!" he cried. "Look at these pictures of desserts!"

Betsy ran to the table and bent her head over the cookbook. "Oh, don't they look good!" she said.

Billy turned a page. "Oh, Betsy!" he shouted. "Lookie! Here's a recipe for cream puffs."

"Umm, yummy!" said Betsy.

"What do you say we make cream puffs?" said Billy.

"Oh, they would be too hard to make," replied Betsy.

"No, they're not," said Billy. "Look," he added, pointing to the page. "It just takes butter and water and flour, salt and eggs. Bet that isn't any harder than pancakes. Come on, what do you say we make them?"

"I think you ought to ask your daddy first," said Betsy.

"Oh, all right," said Billy. "I'll ask him."

Billy went halfway up the stairs. Then he called out, "Daddy!"

"What is it?" Mr. Porter's voice came from the top of the house.

"Can we make cream puffs?" Billy shouted.

"Make what?" his daddy called back.

"Cream puffs," yelled Billy.

"Sure, sure," Daddy answered.

"See?" said Billy, as the two children returned to the kitchen.

Betsy opened the refrigerator. She took out the butter and the eggs. "How much butter does it say, Billy?"

"It says a quarter of a pound," replied Billy.

"Well, there's only a quarter of a pound here," said Betsy. "Maybe your mother wouldn't want us to use the butter."

"I'll ask Daddy," said Billy.

Billy ran halfway up the stairs again. "Daddy!" he shouted.

"Now what is it?" his daddy called back.

"Can we use the butter?" replied Billy.

"Use what?" called Mr. Porter.

"The butter," shouted Billy.

"Sure, sure," came the voice from the attic.

The children returned again to the kitchen. Billy put the butter and water in a saucepan and put the pan on the stove. Betsy brought a cookie tin from the closet. She greased the tin. "How many cream puffs are we going to make?" she asked.

"Oh, I guess it will be a lot," said Billy, as he measured the flour and salt into a bowl.

When the butter and water were boiling, Billy dumped the contents of the bowl into the sauce-pan and stirred it rapidly, just the way the recipe said to. Then he took it from the stove and added four eggs, one at a time. He beat each one in with the electric beater. When he finished, he said, "Say, Betsy, this isn't going to make very many cream puffs. It's only enough for about two. One for you and one for me."

Betsy looked into the saucepan. "Yepper," she said, "you're right. That won't make more than two."

"Well," said Billy, "guess it will be OK. We'll each have one anyway."

He divided the dough into two equal parts.

One half he put at the top of the cookie tin, the other lump at the bottom. "Gee!" he said. "I thought we would surely have two apiece. I'm getting awfully hungry."

"So am I," said Betsy, as Billy put the pan in the oven.

"Well, let's have some cornflakes and milk while we're waiting for the cream puffs to get done," said Billy.

The children sat down at the kitchen table.

They each ate two bowls of cornflakes with milk. Billy, meanwhile, was reading the cookbook. Suddenly he looked up. "Hey, Betsy!" he said. "This cookbook is crazy."

"What do you mean, 'It's crazy'?" asked Betsy.

"Well, it says here, 'This recipe will make twelve good-size cream puffs or thirty-six small ones,' " Billy read.

"It's crazy," said Betsy. "It only makes two."

When the children finished their cornflakes, Billy said, "I guess we better look at them. It's been fifteen minutes."

He opened the oven door and the two children stooped down and looked inside. To their astonishment, there in the oven sat two golden pumpkins. They were the cream puffs, all blown up and six times as big as an ordinary cream puff and eighteen times as big as a small cream puff.

The children's eyes looked as though they were about to fall out onto the kitchen floor.

"Golly!" cried Billy. "I didn't know that they were going to blow up like balloons."

"Jimminy!" cried Betsy. "I'll bet we've made the biggest cream puffs that were ever baked."

"You betcha!" said Billy, closing the oven

door. "It says to turn down the heat and leave them in twenty minutes. Boy! I can hardly wait to eat it."

"Me too," said Betsy.

The children proceeded to wash up the dishes. "We have to get this place cleaned up before Mother comes home," said Billy.

"Yes," replied Betsy, looking at the batter that was still spread over the floor.

Just as Billy took the cream puffs out of the oven his daddy walked into the kitchen.

Billy placed the tin on the table.

"For goodness' sake!" said Mr. Porter. "What are those things?"

"Cream puffs!" exclaimed Billy with pride.

"Cream puffs!" cried his daddy. "Who are they for, pray tell? An elephant?"

"They're for us," said Billy.

"Why didn't you make big ones?" asked his daddy. "And by the way, who, I would like to know, gave you permission to make cream puffs?"

"Why, you did, Daddy," said Billy.

"I did!" exclaimed Daddy. "When did I ever give you permission to make cream puffs?"

"I called upstairs to you, Daddy," replied Billy.

Mr. Porter turned to Betsy. "What about this, Betsy?" he asked. "What's your story?"

"That's right, Mr. Porter," said Betsy. "I heard you. You said, 'Sure, sure.' "

Mr. Porter scratched his nose. "Well, that sounds like me," he said. Then he turned to Billy. "What did you make them of?"

Billy said, "Oh, butter and . . ."

"Butter!" cried Mr. Porter. "You used the butter?"

"But you said we could," replied Billy.

"When did I ever say you could use the butter?" demanded Mr. Porter.

"I called to you, Daddy," said Billy.

"Yes, Mr. Porter," said Betsy, "and you said . . ."

"Never mind, never mind, Betsy," interrupted Mr. Porter. "Don't tell me, I can guess."

Just then Billy looked out of the window and saw his mother turning in the drive.

"Excuse me, Daddy," he said. "I gotta go upstairs."

But his daddy saw his mother coming, too. "No, you don't!" he said, catching hold of Billy.

"But I gotta go upstairs, Daddy," pleaded Billy.

"No, sir," said Daddy. "You're going to stay right here and face the music."

"Hello!" called Mrs. Porter from the front hall. "What's going on?"

"We're all here, Mother," called Mr. Porter. "We've been making cream puffs."

When Mrs. Porter saw the cream puffs, she couldn't help laughing. "They're a little bit small, aren't they?" she said.

"Well, it was the best they could do in this size oven. We'll have to get a bigger oven if these children are going to do very much cooking," said Mr. Porter with a twinkle in his eye. "They seem to have big ideas."

"What is all over the floor?" asked Mrs. Porter.

"Pancakes," said Billy. "The handle broke off of the pitcher."

"And what is all over Betsy?" asked Mrs. Porter.

"That's pancakes, too," said Billy.

"I slipped," said Betsy.

"Well, you two children get the mop and the floor cloth and clean up the floor. I'll take off my hat and make the filling for these giant cream puffs."

"What do you mean, 'filling'?" said Billy. "Aren't they cream puffs?"

"They will be when they are filled with custard," replied Mrs. Porter.

Billy leaned against the table and looked at the results of their baking. "What?" he said. "I thought they were sure 'nough cream puffs now."

Then he ran to the foot of the stairs. "Oh, Mother," he called, "am I going to eat it all myself?"

"You are not," replied his mother.

And Betsy heard Mr. Porter say to himself, "Good thing he didn't ask me. I would have said, 'Sure, sure.' "

2

Names Are Funny Sometimes

After the pancake and cream puff experience, Billy began calling Betsy "Pancake" and Betsy called Billy "Cream Puff."

At first, Billy didn't mind. He just thought it was funny. But when the Wilson boys, who lived around the corner from Billy, heard Betsy call Billy Cream Puff, they screamed with laughter.

There were four Wilson boys: Eddie, aged

seven; the twins, Joe and Frank, who were nine; and Rudy, who was eleven.

"Cream Puff!" they yelled. "What a name for a boy! Hiya! Cream Puff!"

Billy's face got very red. He turned to Betsy. "Now, look what you did," he cried.

"Well, you called me Pancake first," said Betsy.

"Aw, Pancake is just funny. But Cream Puff!" wailed Billy. "It's awful!" And he ran inside the house.

Angry tears were in his eyes. When his mother saw him, she said, "Why, Billy! What's the matter?"

"Oh, Betsy started to call me Cream Puff and those Wilson kids heard her, and now they're calling me Cream Puff and making fun of me," replied Billy.

"Well now, don't pay any attention to them, Billy," said his mother. "Just act as though you didn't care and soon they'll forget about it."

"But no fella wants to be called a sissy name like Cream Puff. And I'll hit the first one who calls me that. I'll just hit him and knock him down."

"Is that so?" said Mrs. Porter. "Well, that's the way savages behave. They knock each other down. But I thought I heard you telling Daddy the other night that you were civilized."

"Well, I *am* civilized," said Billy.

"Well, when you're civilized, you think things out," said his mother. "You decide what is the best way to behave towards people. You don't go up and punch them in the nose."

Billy sat down in a chair and sulked. He could hear Betsy and the Wilson boys playing outside. They were playing with an old football.

Pretty soon Billy grew tired of sitting still. He wanted to go out to play. Finally he jumped up and ran out of the front door.

"Hiya, Cream Puff!" shouted Rudy, the moment Billy appeared. "Catch this."

Billy paid no attention to the name. He caught the ball as it came through the air.

"Let's have it here, Cream Puff," yelled Joe.

Billy kicked the ball. "That ball is a mess," he said.

"It's all worn out," said Betsy. "It won't hold any air."

"It's better than none," replied Rudy. "It's all right to practice with until we get a good one. I'm going to get up a football team."

"Can I be on it?" asked Billy.

"Sure, Puff. You can be on it," said Rudy.

"Can I?" yelled the twins together.

"Yep," replied Rudy.

"Can I be on the team?" asked Eddie.

"No, you're too little," replied Rudy. Whereupon Eddie began to cry and went home.

"What about me?" said Betsy.

"Nix," replied Rudy. "Who ever heard of a girl on a football team?"

"Girls can do anything," said Betsy. "Girls can fly airplanes and drive taxicabs and run streetcars. Why can't they play football?"

"Cause they can't," said Rudy.

"Well, I betcha I'll be on the team," said Betsy.

"Betcha won't," said Rudy. Then he called to Billy, who had the ball. "Come on, Puff, let's see you make a forward pass."

Soon all of the Wilson boys were calling Billy Puff. Billy thought this was much better than Cream Puff. After all, no one would know what it meant. Big strong things puffed. Like locomotives and the wolf that "huffed and puffed until he blew the house down."

No, thought Billy, *it isn't bad to be called Puff*. In fact, he thought Puff Porter sounded more

grown-up than Billy Porter. Lots of the big boys in the school had nicknames like Spike or Butch or Skinny.

By the time Betsy and the Wilson boys went home, Billy was quite pleased with his new name.

That night at dinner Billy said, "Daddy, did you know that I have a nickname?"

"Is that so?" said Daddy. "What is it? Pud?"

"No. It's Puff," replied Billy.

"Puff! Why Puff?" asked Daddy.

"Well, you know how big strong things puff, like locomotives and the wolf that huffed and puffed," said Billy, throwing out his chest. "That's me. Puff Porter."

"Well, well," said his daddy. "Names are funny things."

"Yes," said Billy. "Do you know what we call Betsy?"

"Haven't an idea," said Mr. Porter.

"We call her Pancake," said Billy; and he threw back his head and laughed. "Pancake! I named her that. I'll bet nobody ever had the name Pancake before."

"Does sound a bit unusual," said Daddy. "Does Betsy mind being called Pancake?"

"No," laughed Billy. "She thinks it's funny. Every time I call her that we just laugh and laugh. We always remember about slipping in the pancake batter."

When Betsy reached home, Mother said, "Oh, Betsy, I have just heard that there is to be a new teacher at your school and she is to teach your class."

"You did, Mother!" said Betsy. "What's her name?"

Mother laughed. "Well, Betsy, she has a very unusual name. In fact, I have never known anyone with the same name."

"What is it?" said Betsy.

"Miss Pancake," replied Mother.

Betsy fell into the nearest chair. She rocked from side to side, laughing. "Oh, Mother! You're just fooling. That's what Billy calls me—Pancake."

Mother was laughing too. "No, Betsy, I'm not fooling. That really is her name."

"But I'll never be able to call her Miss Pancake without laughing," said Betsy.

"You will have to learn to say it without laughing, dear. You can't be rude to Miss Pancake."

When Mother said the name, Betsy went off into gales of laughter. "Oh, just wait until I tell Billy," she gasped.

The next morning Betsy was at Billy's house

bright and early. When she told Billy the news about the new teacher, Billy didn't believe it.

"You're just making that up," he said.

"No, I am not," said Betsy. "It's her real name."

"But I can't call her Miss Pancake," chortled Billy. "I'll laugh and laugh."

"That's what I told Mother," said Betsy. "But Mother says that would be rude and that we will have to practice saying it until we can say it without laughing."

The opening day of school was only five days off, so Betsy and Billy had to learn quickly to say Miss Pancake and keep their faces straight.

Every morning when Betsy came downstairs to breakfast, her mother would say, "Good morning, Betsy," and Betsy would reply, "Good morning, Miss Pancake."

The first two mornings she did very badly, for she laughed right in the middle of it.

Over at Billy's house, Mrs. Porter was doing the same thing and Billy was trying to say, "Good morning, Miss Pancake," without exploding. But by the day school opened the children had reached the place where they could say it with only a smile.

They wondered what Miss Pancake would look like. Betsy didn't think she would be pretty. Billy thought she would be tall and thin.

When the children went into their classroom, there, at the front of the room, stood a roly-poly little person with short red curly hair and eyes that looked like black buttons. Betsy noticed that they were very shiny and that they looked very happy.

When all of the children were seated, the teacher said in a voice that chuckled, "Now, boys and girls, I am going to tell you something that is going to make you laugh. I am going to tell you my name, and it is a very funny name. It's Miss Pancake."

The children laughed and laughed and Miss Pancake laughed too. And when she laughed, she seemed to bounce up and down.

Betsy knew, right then and there, that she was going to love Miss Pancake.

It was a happy day and when the children said "Miss Pancake" and laughed, Miss Pancake laughed too.

When school was over, Billy waited by his new teacher's desk until all of the children had gone. Then he said, "Miss Pancake, I've got a funny name too. They call me Puff. Puff Porter."

"That *is* a funny name," said Miss Pancake, with her eyes twinkling. "Why do they call you Puff?"

"Well," replied Billy, "it's a secret, but I'll tell you. It's really Cream Puff."

And Miss Pancake and Billy both threw back their heads and laughed long and loud.

3

Eenie, Meenie, Minie, and Mo

A t the close of the first day of school, Betsy
thought of her old friend, Mr. Kilpatrick.
He was the policeman who took the children
across the wide avenue not very far from the
school.

Father had driven Betsy to school in the morning, so Betsy hadn't seen Mr. Kilpatrick. Now
she skipped along, thinking how nice it would

be to see him. When she turned the next corner, she would be able to see his bright red car parked at the curb.

Sure enough, when Betsy turned the corner, there, away down the street, was Mr. Kilpatrick's car. As she got nearer, she could hear the sharp sound of his whistle. When she reached the corner, Mr. Kilpatrick was in the middle of the street directing the traffic. The moment he saw her his face broke into a big smile. As he came toward her he said, "Well, if it isn't Little Red Ribbons! Sure, it's good to see the little girl again."

"Hello, Mr. Kilpatrick!" said Betsy. "How are you?"

"I couldn't be better," replied Mr. Kilpatrick. "And how do you find yourself?"

"Just fine," said Betsy. "What do you think, Mr. Kilpatrick? My new teacher's name is Miss Pancake."

"Sure, I've been hearing about her," said Mr. Kilpatrick. "It's a good hearty name, isn't it? Goes right to your stomach."

Betsy laughed as Mr. Kilpatrick walked across the street with her. "How is Mrs. Kilpatrick?" asked Betsy.

"She's feeling quite smart," said the policeman. "She'll be asking after you when I get home. She's never forgotten you getting lost when you were back in the first grade."

"That was funny, wasn't it?" said Betsy.

"We have a new cat," said Mr. Kilpatrick. "We call her the Queen of Sheba. And what do you think she carried into the kitchen the other night?"

"I don't know," said Betsy. "What?"

Mr. Kilpatrick leaned over. "A kitten," he said. "Had it in her mouth. Then we found that she had three others. We've put them in a box in the laundry."

"Oh, Mr. Kilpatrick!" cried Betsy. "I would love to see them."

"Well, let's see," said Mr. Kilpatrick, looking at his watch. "My time is about up here. Suppose I drive you around to my house to see them. Then I can run you home."

"That would be lovely," said Betsy.

Mr. Kilpatrick helped Betsy into his red police car. He climbed into the driver's seat and they started off.

"Well," said Mr. Kilpatrick, "how is your friend Billy these days? I didn't see him this morning."

"No, Father drove us both to school this morning. Billy's all right. We had a lovely summer vacation. But do you know what, Mr. Kilpatrick?"

"What?" asked Mr. Kilpatrick.

"I don't think Billy is going to play with me very much now," said Betsy.

"Sure and why not?" asked Mr. Kilpatrick.

"Well, all he wants to do is play football with the Wilson boys," said Betsy.

"What's stopping you from playing with them?" asked Mr. Kilpatrick.

"Oh, they won't let me play," said Betsy. "Rudy says girls can't play football."

"Nonsense!" exclaimed Mr. Kilpatrick. "You'd be as good as the rest of them."

"Well, they won't let me," sighed Betsy.

"Who owns the football?" asked Mr. Kilpatrick.

"Oh, the football!" laughed Betsy. "You should see it. It belongs to Rudy, but it's so old the air won't stay in it."

Mr. Kilpatrick snorted. "Looks to me as though they wouldn't play much football until they get a ball," he said.

"They talk a lot about getting a ball," said Betsy.

"Sure, talk's cheap," said Mr. Kilpatrick.

They drove another block in silence. Then Mr. Kilpatrick said, "I suppose if anyone were to bring out a football, they'd be glad to play with that one. Even if it was one with pigtails and red ribbons."

"Maybe," said Betsy.

And now the car stopped in front of Mr. Kilpatrick's house. Betsy jumped out and Mr. Kilpatrick opened the front gate for her. She walked up the path with its border of bright flowers. Mr. Kilpatrick opened the front door and called, "Hello, Katie!"

Betsy heard Mrs. Kilpatrick's voice from upstairs. "I'm up here, Pat."

"Well, come down," shouted Mr. Kilpatrick. "I've brought an old friend home with me."

Betsy heard Mrs. Kilpatrick's heavy tread above, for the policeman's wife was a large lady. "Now who have you brought with you?" she said.

Mrs. Kilpatrick was at the head of the stairs now. She peered down. "Land sakes!" she cried. "If it isn't the little girl that was lost back in the first grade. There was I, sweeping the pavement and she comes up to me, looking for all the world like a stray puppy." All of this Mrs. Kilpatrick said as she came lumbering down the stairs.

"Well, it's good to see you again," she said. "Did Pat bring you to see the kittens?"

"Yes," replied Betsy. "And the Queen of Sheba, too."

"Well, come right out to the laundry," said Mrs. Kilpatrick.

Betsy followed Mrs. Kilpatrick to the back of the house. In the doorway between the kitchen and the laundry sat the biggest and most beautiful cat Betsy had ever seen. It was the Queen of Sheba. She was coal black and her yellow eyes were like big amber beads.

"She doesn't like you to touch her babies," said Mrs. Kilpatrick. "Come on here, Queen of Sheba. You go outside for a while."

Mrs. Kilpatrick opened the back door. The Queen of Sheba sat like a statue, looking at her.

"Come on here; don't put on any of your haughty airs with me," said Mrs. Kilpatrick. "Out with you!"

The Queen of Sheba didn't even blink.

"Do you see that?" said Mrs. Kilpatrick. "Majestic, I calls it. Majestic."

Mrs. Kilpatrick reached for her broom. "Now, Your Majesty, will you git? Or shall I help you?"

The Queen of Sheba got. She got, majestically, out of the back door.

"Now come look at the kittens," said Mrs. Kilpatrick, leading Betsy toward the box in the corner.

"Oh!" cried Betsy. But Mrs. Kilpatrick interrupted. "Sakes alive!" she cried. "There's one of them missing! Now what did that cat do with that kitten?"

Betsy went down on her knees beside the box. She looked down at the three furry little balls. "Aren't they sweet!" she said.

"Sure, but where's the fourth one?" said Mrs. Kilpatrick, looking all around the laundry. "You know, the Queen's got a grudge against that kitten. That's the second time she's carried it off.

Last time I found it in the coal bucket beside the fireplace."

Mrs. Kilpatrick tramped into the front room. Betsy followed her to the coal bucket.

"Well, she's not put it in the coal bucket this time," said Mrs. Kilpatrick.

Betsy started to look under the furniture while Mrs. Kilpatrick picked up the sofa cushions.

"What color is it?" asked Betsy.

"It's a yellow one," said Mrs. Kilpatrick. "The only one in the litter that wasn't like the mother. I declare, it's just as though the Queen didn't like the kitten because it's different from her and the rest of them."

"Sort of an ugly duckling?" said Betsy.

"That's it!" replied Mrs. Kilpatrick. "But you remember the ugly duckling turned out to be the beauty of the lot, and it's my opinion that this kitten will be the beauty, too. Now where do you suppose that cat hid that kitten?"

Mrs. Kilpatrick's sewing basket was on a low stool. Betsy looked into the basket. It was filled with Mr. Kilpatrick's socks and shirts that needed mending. But curled up in the center of the basket was a round golden ball of soft fur. "Here it is!" cried Betsy.

Mrs. Kilpatrick leaned over the basket. "Well, sure as faith! You've found it," she cried. Picking it up, she placed it in Betsy's arms.

Betsy carried the kitten back to the laundry. "What have you named them?" she asked.

"They're not named yet," said Mrs. Kilpatrick. "Have you any ideas about names?"

Betsy was delighted. She loved naming things.

"Well," she said, "first of all, are they boys or girls?"

"Sure, I guess only time will tell," said Mrs. Kilpatrick. "It's hard to tell when they're so young."

"Of course," said Betsy, "their mother being a Queen, they will be princes and princesses."

"Now I never thought of that," said Mrs. Kilpatrick. "But of course you're right. Princesses and princes they are."

"It would be funny," said Betsy, "if you gave them girls' names, like Princess Mabel or Princess Katherine, and then they turned out to be boys. Prince Mabel or Prince Katherine would sound awfully funny."

Mrs. Kilpatrick and Betsy both laughed. "That's right," said Mrs. Kilpatrick. "It would probably have a bad effect on their dispositions."

Betsy puckered up her brow and looked down at the kittens. She was still holding the yellow one. Finally she looked up at Mrs. Kilpatrick. "I know what!" she cried, and her eyes were shining. "We could call them Eenie, Meenie, Minie, and Mo. Then when they get bigger it won't make any difference whether they are Prince Eenie or Princess Eenie or Prince Meenie or Princess Meenie or Prince Minie or Princess Minie or Prince Mo or Princess Mo."

Mrs. Kilpatrick clapped her hands together. "Now that's what I call right smart," she said. "What do you want to call the one you are holding?"

Betsy looked at the kitten. "I think this one should be Eenie," she said. "And the black ones can be Meenie, Minie, and Mo."

"Well now, that's right elegant!" said Mrs. Kilpatrick. "And how would you like to have Eenie for your own kitten?"

"Oh, that would be wonderful!" exclaimed Betsy. "You mean I can take him home and keep him?"

"Certainly," said Mrs. Kilpatrick.

"Oh, I wonder if Thumpy would mind," said Betsy. "Thumpy is my cocker spaniel, you know."

"Well, Thumpy couldn't treat that kitten any worse than its own mother treats it," said Mrs. Kilpatrick.

"That's right," said Betsy. "I guess Thumpy would get used to it."

"Do you think your father and mother would have any objection to your having a kitten?" asked Mrs. Kilpatrick.

"Oh, no!" said Betsy. "Mother and Father said I could have one, if I could get a nice one. And this is a very nice one," she added, holding the kitten up. "I didn't expect to get a member of a royal family."

"Where do you suppose Pat got to?" said Mrs. Kilpatrick. "I forgot all about him."

"I think he went upstairs," said Betsy, as she followed Mrs. Kilpatrick back into the front room.

Mrs. Kilpatrick went to the foot of the stairs. "Pat!" she called. "Where are you?"

"I'm coming. Right away," Mr. Kilpatrick called back.

"He's probably rummaging," said Mrs. Kilpatrick. "Loves to get up in the attic and rummage. Like as not he'll come downstairs with something I haven't seen in years."

Betsy sat down on a chair to wait for Mr. Kilpatrick. Soon she heard a door bang.

"Didn't I tell you?" said Mrs. Kilpatrick. "He's been in the attic. Now watch if I didn't speak the truth. Sure as my name's Katie, he'll be carrying something under his arm, and like as not I'll have to carry it back again."

In a few moments Mr. Kilpatrick began descending the stairs. As Betsy looked up, she saw first his feet; then his legs; and then the part of Mr. Kilpatrick that his belt went 'round, and that was a very big part. When his arms came into view, Betsy saw to her amazement that under one arm Mr. Kilpatrick carried a football.

"Now, Little Red Ribbons," said Mr. Kilpatrick, when he got all the way downstairs. "I've a football here. Do you think, by any chance, it would be useful to you?"

Betsy's eyes were like dollars. "Oh, Mr. Kilpatrick!" she cried, jumping up. "Do you mean that you are giving it to me?"

"That was my idea," said Mr. Kilpatrick. "But you must be very canny about it."

"What do you mean, 'canny'?" asked Betsy.

"I mean you mustn't let the boys know that you've got a football until you're sure that they'll let you play. Let them worry a little bit about getting a football. In other words, 'keep it up your sleeve.' "

"It's awful big to go up my sleeve," said Betsy with a twinkle.

Mr. Kilpatrick laughed his great big laugh. "What I mean is, you must keep it all hidden. You mustn't let on to the boys that you have it."

"I know," said Betsy, laughing. "That will be fun, won't it?"

"I think it will be," said Mr. Kilpatrick; "quite a lot of fun. And now I'll wrap it up and take you home."

Betsy said good-bye to Mrs. Kilpatrick and thanked her for the kitten. Mr. Kilpatrick put her into the car. In her arms she held the kitten. The football, hidden away in a hatbox, sat on her lap.

On her way home Betsy said, "Thank you very much for the football, Mr. Kilpatrick."

And Mr. Kilpatrick said, "You're very welcome, little one. It was my boy's football many years ago. I've taken good care of it. He's in the Navy now. He'd be surprised to know that I gave his football to a little girl."

"Won't he mind?" asked Betsy.

"Sure, he won't mind a bit," said Mr. Kilpatrick. "He'll enjoy the joke on the boys."

Betsy looked up at Mr. Kilpatrick and her whole face twinkled. "Oh, Mr. Kilpatrick," she said, "won't Billy be surprised when he finds out that I have a football up my sleeve?"

4

It's a Secret

When Betsy stepped out of Mr. Kilpatrick's red car, she heard Billy call, "Hiya, Betsy!"

"Oh, dear! There's Billy," said Betsy to Mr. Kilpatrick. "He's on our side porch."

"Good thing we put that football in the hatbox," whispered Mr. Kilpatrick. "He'll never guess what it is."

Betsy giggled. "Wouldn't he be surprised if

he knew?" she whispered back. Aloud she said, "Thank you, Mr. Kilpatrick, for bringing me home."

By this time Billy had run out to the car. "Hello, Mr. Kilpatrick!" he cried. "Why did you have to bring Betsy home?"

Then he spied the kitten in Betsy's arms. "Oh, boy!" he cried. "Where did you get the swell kitten?" Billy's eyes were big and round.

"Mrs. Kilpatrick gave it to me. It's a royal prince or princess. We don't know which. But anyway its mother is the Queen of Sheba."

"Golly!" exclaimed Billy.

"Well, so long," called Mr. Kilpatrick as he started the car. "Careful of your hat, Betsy," he added with a grin.

"Good-bye, Mr. Kilpatrick," said Betsy. "Thanks for everything."

Billy followed Betsy into the house and out onto the porch. Betsy placed the hatbox on a chair and sat down with the kitten.

"What's the kitten's name?" asked Billy.

"Eenie," said Betsy.

"Eenie?" replied Billy. "That's a funny name."

"No, it's a good name," said Betsy. " 'Cause if it's Eenie, it can be either a prince or a princess."

Billy stroked the kitten. "Gee! I wish I could have one. Are there any more?"

"Yes, there are Meenie, Minie, and Mo. But they are all black, like the Queen of Sheba," said Betsy, putting the kitten on the floor.

Billy sat down on the chair beside the hatbox. He looked at the kitten fondly. "Do you suppose Mrs. Kilpatrick would let me have one of them?" asked Billy, leaning his elbow on the box.

"I don't know," replied Betsy. " 'Course I didn't ask for this kitten. Mrs. Kilpatrick offered it to me."

Billy began twiddling with the string on the box. "Guess it wouldn't be polite to ask for one, would it?" he said.

"Oh, no!" said Betsy, keeping her eye on the box.

"Maybe she would sell one," said Billy as his fingers took hold of the bow of the string.

"Well, maybe," said Betsy.

"But I haven't any money," said Billy, plucking at the bow. It made a drumming sound on the lid of the box.

"I thought you were going to play football this afternoon," said Betsy.

"The football has caloopsed," said Billy.

"What do you mean, 'caloopsed'?" asked Betsy.

"It's n.g.—no good. Collapsed, in plain English," replied Billy.

"Oh!" said Betsy.

"We have to find a way to buy a new one," said Billy, still plucking at the bow. "That's why I couldn't buy a kitten. I have to save my money for a football."

"Oh!" said Betsy. And just as she said it the bow on the hatbox came untied.

Betsy jumped up so suddenly that she startled Billy and he knocked the hatbox off the chair. It fell to the floor with a thud and rolled across the porch. Betsy's heart was in her mouth, but fortunately the lid stuck fast. Both of the children ran after the box but Betsy reached it first. She picked it up with her hand firmly against the lid and quickly tied the string in a knot.

"What's in the box?" asked Billy. "A new hat?"

"No," replied Betsy. "It isn't a new hat. I guess I'll take it upstairs."

Betsy picked up the box by the string. "You mind Eenie," she said, "until I come back."

"OK," Billy replied.

Betsy went into the house and started upstairs. She didn't notice that the bottom of the box had cracked when it fell off the chair. When she reached the top of the stairs the bottom of the box suddenly gave way, and the football fell out. It struck the step and bounced, the crooked way all footballs bounce, hither and thither, all the way down the steps. Then, to Betsy's horror, it rolled into the living room. She could hear Billy's chair squeak as he jumped out of it. "Hey!" he cried. "What's the matter?" But just then Thumpy, Betsy's cocker spaniel, dashed through the living room and out on the porch. "Oh, golly-wops!" Betsy heard Billy cry. "Here, Thumpy, you leave that kitten alone."

By this time Betsy had reached the football, which had rolled almost to the porch door. As she dashed upstairs with it she could hear Billy yelling, "Thumpy, get down! Get down, Thumpy! Stop it, Thumpy!"

And Betsy thought, "Good old Thumpy!" as she stowed the football away in her closet.

When Betsy returned to the porch she found Billy holding the kitten as high as he could, out of Thumpy's reach. Thumpy was leaping up and down and throwing himself against Billy.

"Get down, Thumpy," said Betsy. "Down!"

Thumpy stopped leaping and stood with his

pink tongue hanging out and his tail wagging. Betsy took the kitten from Billy.

"He was going to fight it," said Billy.

"Don't be silly," said Betsy. "Thumpy wouldn't fight a kitten. He's just glad to see the kitten, that's all."

Betsy held the kitten down, so that Thumpy could see it. Thumpy let out pleased little barks.

"They're going to be good friends," said Betsy.

At this moment Lucy, the cook, appeared in the doorway. "I just come to see what was all the racket on the stairs," she said.

"Oh, the bottom fell out of my hatbox," replied Betsy.

"Sure made a lot of noise," said Lucy. "I thought you was playing ball where 'taint allowed."

"That's what I thought it sounded like too, Lucy," said Billy.

Just then Betsy's mother came in the front door with Betsy's little sister, Star. Betsy ran to meet them.

"Mother!" she called. "Come out on the porch and see my kitten. Mrs. Kilpatrick gave it to me."

"Why, Betsy!" exclaimed Mother. "How lovely

of Mrs. Kilpatrick! Come, Star, let's see Betsy's kitty."

When Star saw the kitten she went down on all fours so that she could see it better.

Betsy was so busy watching Star and the kitten that she didn't see Lucy standing in the doorway.

"Betsy!" said Lucy.

Betsy looked up. There stood Lucy with the remains of the hatbox. "What this old box doin' on the stairs?"

"I don't want it, Lucy," said Betsy. "Please throw it away."

"What you bring it home for anyway?" said Lucy. "What all was in it?"

Betsy rushed toward Lucy. "I don't want it,

Lucy," she said, gently pushing Lucy into the living room. "Throw it away, please."

"Beats everything," muttered Lucy. "Always bringing good-for-nothing junk into the house."

"Darling," said Mother, turning to Betsy, "why did you bring that old box home? You know it just makes work for Lucy."

"It wasn't an old box when I brought it home, Mother. It was a good box," replied Betsy. "Look, Mother. Isn't the kitten cute?"

They all played with the kitten until, at last, Father came home. "Hello, there!" he called. "What's going on?"

"We've a kitten," Betsy said as she ran to kiss Father.

"Well! Well!" said Father, looking at the kitten. "Quite a beauty, isn't it?"

Father and Mother left the children on the porch. Mother went into the kitchen to talk to Lucy and Father went upstairs. When Father reached the head of the stairs, he picked up the lid of the hatbox. "Now, I'll bet Thumpy has gotten my hatbox," he muttered to himself. "Now where do you suppose my good hat is? I'll have to speak to Betsy about this."

Father came out on the porch with the lid of the hatbox.

"Betsy!" he said, "do you know anything about the box that belongs to this lid?"

"Yes, Father," replied Betsy. "Lucy threw it away."

"Well, what was in the box?" asked Father.

"There wasn't anything in the box. It was empty and Lucy threw it away," Betsy said.

"But what was in the box before Lucy threw it away?" asked Father.

Betsy gulped. "Why, uh . . . Why, Father," she said, pushing past him through the door. "Why, uh . . ." By this time she was in the living room and out of sight of Billy. She motioned to Father to lean over. Then she whispered in his ear, "I'll tell you after a while. It's a secret."

Father made a funny face and tiptoed out of the room. He put the box lid on his head, and when he reached the doorway he tipped it to Betsy. Betsy doubled up, laughing. Then she went out on the porch again.

"I guess I had better be going," said Billy. "It sure is a nice kitten. If I didn't have to save my money to buy a football, I would ask Mr. Kilpatrick if he would sell one of the other kittens to me. But I guess you can't have a kitten and a football, both."

"I guess you can't," said Betsy.

Billy looked at the kitten very thoughtfully. "Well," he said, "I guess I would rather have a football."

By this time the children had reached the front door.

Suddenly Betsy realized that Mother was in Betsy's room. She heard Mother open the closet door. Then Mother's voice called, "Betsy! Whose ball is this?"

Betsy opened the front door and pushed Billy out.

"What kind of a ball is it?" said Billy.

"Oh, it's a ball," replied Betsy. "You know. A ball."

"Oh, a ball!" said Billy.

"That's right," said Betsy. "A ball. See you tomorrow."

Betsy closed the door with a sigh of relief. Then she dashed upstairs. "Oh, Mother!" she said. "It's mine. Mr. Kilpatrick gave it to me and it's a secret from Billy."

"Oh!" said Mother. "I am so sorry, Betsy. I didn't know."

"Well, I didn't know it could be so hard to keep a secret," said Betsy.

5

How to Get a Football

R udy Wilson and his football team were in
a bad way, because you can't play football
without a ball. And their ball was a sorry-looking
sight.

One day Rudy sent the word around to the
boys on the team that there would be a meeting
of the team after school. They were to meet on
the vacant lot next to Billy's house. Rudy said

that he had very important business to discuss.

By four o'clock, Billy and the Wilson twins, together with Kenny and Christopher, Richard and Henry, were gathered in a bunch. They were waiting for Rudy.

Soon little Eddie Wilson came trotting up to the group of boys. "What's going on?" he asked.

No one paid any attention to him. He pulled at Billy's sleeve. "Hey, Puff!" he said. "What's going on?"

"We're going to have a business meeting," replied Billy.

"What kind of business?" asked Eddie.

"Oh, it's about the team," said Billy. "You run along and play."

"I don't wanta play," said Eddie. "I wanta be on the team."

"Well, you can't be on the team," said Billy. "We told you that before. You're too little."

"Well, I'm going to stay," said Eddie. "And you can't put me off this lot. 'Cause you don't own it." Eddie sat down firmly on the ground.

"You'll have to get out of here when Rudy comes," said Billy.

"Nope," said Eddie. "I'm gonna be on the team."

In a few minutes Rudy arrived. He was out of breath from running. He had a magazine in his hand.

"Now, fellas," he said, waving the magazine, "we've got two important things to decide. First of all, we have to get a football and next we have to get a name for the team."

"Let's be the Tigers," said Kenny.

"Naw," said Rudy, "there are lots of teams called the Tigers. We have to be different."

"How about the Wildcats?" said Billy.

"Not bad," said Rudy. "But we ought to have something different."

"How about the Mad Alligators?" piped up little Eddie.

Rudy looked around at Eddie and saw him squatting on the ground.

"Eddie," he said, "scram! You're not on the team, and you'll never be on the team, so you can't attend the business meetings. You go away and play."

Eddie began to cry. "I wanta be on the team," he sobbed.

"Frank!" Rudy called. "Take Eddie home."

"I won't go home," screamed Eddie.

Just then Betsy appeared on Billy's side porch.

"Billy," she called, "what are you doing?"

"We're having a business meeting of the football team," he called back.

"Have you got a football?" yelled Betsy.

"Not yet," Billy shouted back. "But we're going to get one soon."

Then Rudy had an idea. "Hey, Betsy!" he called. "Come here."

Betsy came across the lot to the boys. Rudy went to meet her.

"Say, Betsy," he said, "if you'll take Eddie off and play with him while we have our business meeting, you can be the Grand Matron of the team."

"What does the Grand Matron mean?" asked Betsy.

"Oh, the Grand Matron is very important," replied Rudy. "You can wear the insignia of the team on an arm band."

"Can I play football?" asked Betsy.

"You can be the cheerleader," said Rudy.

"Huh!" said Betsy. "I don't want to be cheerleader. And, what's more, there won't be anybody to cheer. You don't even have a football."

"Well, we're going to get one," said Rudy. "I know a dandy way to get one."

By this time Betsy and Rudy had reached the group of boys. Eddie was still wiping tears out of his eyes with a dirty little fist.

"Come on, Eddie," said Betsy, "let's go have a party on Billy's porch. I brought some cookies over from my house and Mrs. Porter is making some lemonade."

Without another tear Eddie trotted off with Betsy.

"Hurry up, Rudy," said Billy. "Get this business meeting over. I've got something important to do at home."

"Well," said Rudy, "maybe it would be better if we finished the meeting on your porch. Maybe it would be more comfortable."

"That's right," said Christopher. "We could sit down on Puff's porch."

"Gee, yes!" said Joe. "I'm tired of standing around here."

"So am I," said Henry.

"It's cooler on Puff's porch," said Richard.

"That's right," agreed Frank.

"But Betsy and Eddie will hear all our private business," said Billy.

"Oh, well, that's all right," said Rudy. "I just made Betsy Grand Matron of the team anyway."

"But what about Eddie?" asked Billy.

"Well, we can make him the mascot," said Rudy.

With this, the whole bunch set off at top speed for Billy's porch. When they arrived, Betsy and Eddie were already munching cookies and drinking lemonade.

"We've decided to hold the meeting here on the porch," said Billy, looking around for the cookies which were not in sight.

"And, Eddie, we've decided to make you the mascot," said Rudy.

"What's 'at?" asked Eddie.

"Oh, the mascot brings the team good luck," said Rudy.

"Do I run with the ball?" asked Eddie. "And do I kick it?"

"No, no," said Rudy. "You just bring good luck."

"Well, I won't do it," said Eddie, popping the last piece of cookie into his mouth.

"Where are the cookies, Betsy?" asked Billy.

"Oh, I just brought two," said Betsy. "Eddie and I ate them."

The faces of the whole football team fell.

"What kind of cookies were they?" asked Billy.

"Coconut," said Betsy, swallowing her last mouthful.

"Oh! Coconut!" muttered Billy, his mouth fairly watering. And the whole team said, "Oh! Coconut!"

Just then Mrs. Porter appeared at the door with a tray. On it were a pitcher of lemonade and some glasses. "Would you boys like some lemonade?" she asked.

The faces of the team brightened. They were glad that they hadn't missed the whole party.

When the boys were seated with their glasses of lemonade, Rudy said, "Now, fellas, let's get down to business. We have to decide on a name for the team."

"The Mad Alligators," piped up Eddie.

"You keep out of this, Eddie," said Joe. "We have to think of something exciting."

The children sat thinking. The only sound was that of lemonade being poured out of the pitcher. Then gulps and more lemonade poured out of the pitcher.

At last Eddie spoke up again. "Dragons!" he said. "Dragons are 'citing. They're fierce. There's nothing fiercer than dragons."

"Naw!" said the football team in one voice.

Quiet followed.

After a while Billy began to mutter to himself. "Dragons. Dragons. What kind of dragons?"

"Yeh! What kind of dragons?" asked Kenny.

"Purple dragons," said Eddie. "There's nothing fiercer than purple dragons."

"Purple dragons!" said Rudy. "Aw, who ever heard of purple dragons?"

"That's good," said Betsy. "The Purple Dragons. And you could have a purple dragon sewed on your football suit."

"Say, that's swell!" shouted Christopher.

"W-e-l-l, OK!" said Rudy. "All in favor of

calling the team the Purple Dragons, say 'Aye.' "

There was a chorus of "Aye" and Eddie yelled the loudest.

"Now for the next business," said Rudy. "About the football. I've found something wonderful. It's an advertisement in this magazine."

Rudy opened the magazine to the back section of advertisements. His finger ran down the page and stopped. "Here it is," he said. "It says, 'Boys, Win a Football! Finest quality football. Genuine pigskin. The same ball used by college teams. Yours for only a little effort.' "

"Gee! That's great!" said Billy.

"What do you do to get it?" asked Joe.

"Well, this is what it says," said Rudy. He read again from the magazine. " 'Fill out the coupon below with your name and address and we will send you two dozen cakes of Surething Flea Soap, the soap that keeps dogs happy. Send no money.' " Here Rudy stopped and looked at the team. Their faces were pleased and their eyes were bright.

"Oh, boy! That's wonderful!" said Billy.

Rudy went on reading. " 'Send no money,' " he repeated. " 'Your expressman will deliver the soap upon payment of two dollars and forty cents.' "

The faces of the team grew more sober. Rudy cleared his throat and continued. " 'Sell this soap to your friends for twenty cents a cake and send the money to Surething Flea Soap Company and you will receive the genuine pigskin football by return mail. Act quickly! Only a limited supply!' "

"Where are we going to get two dollars and forty cents?" asked Henry. "That's what I want to know."

"With our dues," said Rudy.

"Dues?" said Kenny.

"Sure," said Rudy. "We gotta have dues. Let's see, thirty cents apiece. That will make two dollars and forty cents."

"That's right," said Christopher. "And if we send for it today, it won't be here until some time next week and we'll all have time to pay our dues and raise the money."

"Oh, sure," said Rudy. "Come on, let's fill out the coupon. Where shall we have it sent?"

There was much chatter about whose name and address should be written on the coupon. Finally Rudy said, "Well, as long as we are at your house, Puff, suppose we have it delivered here."

"OK," said Billy.

Rudy filled out the coupon as the rest of the boys crowded around him. He wrote down after the word "Name"—Billy. When Billy saw his, he said, "Not Billy! Here! Let me do it."

Billy took the slip of paper from Rudy and erased the name Billy. Then he wrote down William Porter, Junior, and his address. When he finished, he went upstairs and got an envelope from his daddy's desk.

When the coupon was sealed in the envelope, Rudy said, "I'll mail it on the way home. I have three cents for a stamp."

As the days went by the boys forgot all about their dues to pay for the soap when it arrived. They were too busy thinking about the football.

Once Billy said to his father, "Daddy, our football team is going to get a football."

And Daddy said, "Is that so? Well, that's great."

A few days later Mr. Porter said to Susie who was doing the laundry: "I have ordered some tubes of paint and they should be here today. When the expressman brings the package, pay for it out of this five dollar bill."

"Yes, sir," said Susie.

That very afternoon the expressman rang the doorbell. Susie went to the door. When she opened it, the expressman said, "What's the name?"

"Porter," said Susie. "How much is it?"

"Two-forty," replied the expressman. "Sign here," he said, handing Susie a slip of paper. "Where do you want the box?"

"Set it right here in the hall closet," said Susie. The expressman carried the box into the house and placed it on the floor of the closet.

When Billy came home from school he settled down to a jigsaw puzzle.

Soon Mr. Porter returned.

Susie said, "Mr. Porter, your package came. It's in the hall closet and your change is on the hall table. It was two dollars and forty cents."

"Oh, thank you, Susie," said Mr. Porter.

Billy's daddy went to the hall closet and picked up the box. He carried it upstairs to his studio. Without examining the label, he pried off the lid. There, to his amazement, were two dozen cakes of Surething Flea Soap.

"What the mischief is this!" exclaimed Mr. Porter. "Who is sending me two dozen cakes of flea soap? Two dollars and forty cents' worth of flea soap!"

Then he remembered something that Billy had said about soap. Something about soap and a football. This was a pretty mess! The very idea! Two dollars and forty cents' worth of flea soap! What did Billy intend doing with the stuff?

Mr. Porter went to the head of the stairs.

"William!" he called.

"Yes, Daddy," replied Billy.

"Come up here," said Daddy.

6

Twenty-Four Cakes
of Flea Soap

Billy knew that something was the matter.
Daddy hadn't called him William since the
day last spring when he broke the bathroom window with his baseball. He wondered, as he
climbed the two flights of stairs, what he had
done that would make Daddy call him William.

As he entered his daddy's room, he saw him
standing over a large box.

"William!" said Daddy in a very stern voice, "do you know anything about this soap?"

"Soap?" said Billy.

"Yes. Soap," said Mr. Porter, "Flea soap. In fact, twenty-four cakes of flea soap. Two dollars and forty cents' worth of flea soap. Plus the worst smell in forty-eight states."

"Oh!" said Billy. "Oh! That's our soap."

"Our soap!" exclaimed Daddy. "What are we going to do with it?"

"No, Daddy," said Billy. "You don't understand. It belongs to our football team."

"Well, what I do understand is that I paid two dollars and forty cents for it," said Daddy. "So if it belongs to your football team, I would like to have the money returned to me." And then he added, "Promptly."

"Oh, sure, Daddy. Sure!" said Billy. "I'll call a meeting of the team tomorrow. And I'll bring the money home with me."

And with this Billy dashed for the head of the stairs.

"Hold on a minute," said his daddy. "What in the name of all smells does the team intend doing with this flea soap?"

Billy came back. "Why, we're going to sell

it, Daddy, and get a football. We sell it for twenty cents a cake. Then we get the football."

"Well, get my two dollars and forty cents," said Mr. Porter. "And get rid of this soap as quickly as possible. I'll put it out in the garage. A gas mask should go with each cake."

The following day Billy met Betsy on the way to school.

"Hi, Betsy!" Billy called out. "Our soap has come."

"What soap?" said Betsy.

"Why, the flea soap that the team is going to sell to get the football," said Billy.

"Oh!" replied Betsy. "That soap!"

When the children reached the school, Billy sent word around that there would be a meeting of the football team at recess.

After the opening exercises Miss Pancake put some arithmetic problems on the blackboard and gave each child a piece of paper. Everyone set to work and the room was very quiet. In a few moments Sally, who sat across the aisle from Billy, looked up with a very strange expression on her face. She sniffed. And then she sniffed again.

In a few moments she tiptoed up to the front

of the room and spoke to Miss Pancake in a very low voice.

Miss Pancake said, "Just sit here, at this table by the door."

Sally returned to her seat and got her paper. In a moment she was quietly working at the table by the door.

Very shortly Mary Lou, who sat across the aisle on the other side of Billy, raised her hand.

"What is it, Mary Lou?" asked Miss Pancake.

"May I please sit by the window?" said Mary Lou. "I think I need a little more air."

"Certainly," replied Miss Pancake. And Mary Lou carried her paper over to the desk by the window.

In a few minutes Ellen, who was sitting behind Billy, raised her head from her work. She put her handkerchief to her nose and held it there while she did her problems.

When Miss Pancake looked at her, she said, "Is there anything the matter with your nose, Ellen?"

"I think maybe it would be better if I sat by the window too," replied Ellen.

"Very well," said Miss Pancake. And Ellen moved.

It wasn't long before Betty Jane, who sat in front of Billy, held up her hand.

"What is it, Betty Jane?" said Miss Pancake.

Betty Jane got up and walked up to the teacher's desk. She whispered something to Miss Pancake. Miss Pancake moved a chair over to the table beside Sally and Betty Jane sat down.

By this time Billy, who was busy working out his problems, looked like an island completely surrounded by empty seats.

Miss Pancake stood up and walked down the aisle. She stopped beside Billy's desk. She sniffed.

Then she walked to the back of the room and up the other aisle. When she reached Billy's desk, she stopped again. Then she took out her handkerchief. She looked puzzled.

Just then Christopher looked up from his paper. He wrinkled up his nose and looked around. Then he said, "Gee, Miss Pancake! Something stinks!"

"Christopher!" said Miss Pancake. "I'm surprised at you. That is very vulgar."

"Well, it does, Miss Pancake," said Christopher. "It sure does st— I mean, smells awful. Worse than Limburger cheese."

By this time all of the children were sniffing. "Whew!" they exclaimed.

"Be quiet, children," said Miss Pancake. "Does anyone know what this strange odor is?"

"Oh!" cried Billy, his face as bright as a dollar. "Maybe it's my soap. It's a new kind of flea soap, Miss Pancake. The football team is selling it. Only twenty cents a cake. It makes dogs happy."

"Well, perhaps," said Miss Pancake. "But it certainly is not making this room happy. So suppose you put the soap on the windowsill outside the window."

"All right," said Billy.

"Say!" said Christopher. "I'm not going to sell anything that st— I mean, smells like that. Skunks!"

"Aw, the dogs will like it," said Billy.

Billy put the cake of soap on the windowsill and the little girls returned to their seats around Billy.

"Sissies!" said Billy. "That soap smells good. I would like to take a bath with it myself."

"Well, if you do I hope you'll take it Saturday night," said Ellen.

The soap sat on the windowsill until recess. Then Billy took it and ran off to meet the football team. Soon the boys were gathered together.

"The soap came," cried Billy as soon as Rudy appeared. "I have a cake here. The rest of it is in our garage. My daddy paid for it."

"Gee! That's great!" interrupted Rudy. And the faces of the team lit up.

"But my daddy wants the two dollars and forty cents," said Billy. "So you'll have to collect the dues, Rudy."

The faces of the team grew long.

"OK, OK," said Rudy. "Fellas, hand over your dues."

Eight hands went into eight pockets and all kinds of things came out. Marbles, screws, nails, bits of string, bottle tops, thumbtacks, rubber bands, bits of colored glass, pebbles, seashells, balls of tinfoil, golf balls, wheels from broken toys, and seventeen cents in all.

"Seventeen cents isn't enough," said Billy.

"Well, I don't think we can sell that soap anyway," said Christopher. "It st— you know."

"That's right," said Henry. And Richard, who was Henry's twin, said, "That's right."

"My father says I can't sell soap," said Kenny. "He says he won't allow it."

"Well, say! What am I going to do with all that soap and what about my father's two dollars

and forty cents?" said Billy. "What about that?"

"And what about our football?" said Rudy.

Just then little Eddie appeared. "Whatcha doin'?" said Eddie. "What's up?"

As usual nobody paid any attention to Eddie, so Eddie just hung around trying to pick up the news. It wasn't very long before he understood that Billy was stuck with two dollars and forty cents' worth of flea soap.

Nothing had been settled when the bell rang for the children to return to their classrooms. But it didn't look as though the boys were going to sell any soap.

Billy returned to his room looking very gloomy indeed. When Miss Pancake saw him, she said, "Goodness gracious, Billy! What is the matter?"

Billy told Miss Pancake the whole story about the soap.

"How many boys in the room are on the team?" said Miss Pancake.

A half dozen hands went up.

"Who is captain?" she said.

"Rudy Wilson," replied Billy.

"You boys stay after school for a meeting," said Miss Pancake. "I'll send word to Rudy."

Rudy arrived as soon as the class was dismissed.

"Now," said Miss Pancake to the little boys, "you must work out a way to pay Billy's father the money that you owe him."

"But what about our football?" asked Rudy.

"Most of the boys tell me that they don't want to sell the soap," said Miss Pancake. "So you will have to get your football in some other way."

Just then little Eddie appeared in the open doorway. "What's the matter?" asked Eddie.

"Are you on the team too?" asked Miss Pancake.

"Yes, ma'am," answered Eddie.

"No, he isn't," said Rudy.

"Am," said Eddie and sat down.

"Well now, boys, you will have to think of some way to raise the two dollars and forty cents. I'll write your ideas on the blackboard."

The team sat very still. They were all thinking hard.

Finally Eddie spoke up. "We could wash dogs," he said.

Miss Pancake wrote on the board, "Wash dogs."

"That is a very good idea," she said. "If you charge twenty-five cents each, how many dogs would you have to wash? Billy?"

"Ten," said Billy.

"That's an awful lot of dogs," said Rudy.

The boys sat still for five more minutes. Nothing was added to the blackboard.

At last Miss Pancake said, "Well, is this the only idea?"

The boys looked at each other. "Guess so," they murmured.

"All right!" said Miss Pancake. "Tomorrow is Saturday. You can all spend the day washing dogs."

"Where will we get the dogs?" asked Christopher.

"You will have to go out and find them," said Miss Pancake. "There must be plenty of people who would like to have their dog washed on Saturday morning."

"Where will we wash them?" asked Kenny.

"You will have to decide that," replied Miss Pancake.

"I guess we can wash them in our garage," said Billy. "That's where the soap is."

"Very well," said Miss Pancake. "You can go now, and on Monday morning I want to hear that your debt is paid and that every boy helped. And let this be a lesson to you, Billy. Never sign your name to anything you can't pay for."

"I'll remember, Miss Pancake," said Billy.

The following morning the boys were up bright and early. They scoured the neighborhood for dogs to wash. By nine o'clock Billy was busy washing the next door neighbors' Airedale.

He had just finished when Rudy arrived with a Scottie.

In the middle of the Scottie's bath Kenny came in with an Eskimo dog. Later Christopher brought in a fox terrier.

The dogs behaved very well. It was just as Billy had said. They liked the odor of the soap.

Late in the morning Richard and Henry arrived with their own red setter, Chummy. They set to work on him together.

Just as they finished Billy cried out, "Look what Eddie's bringing!" Billy pointed up the street. The boys looked. Then their mouths fell open. For there, moving majestically beside Eddie, was the biggest dog the boys had ever seen. It was a Saint Bernard.

"Take it away," yelled Rudy.

"We're not washing that dog for twenty-five cents," called out Billy.

"Nix!" yelled Christopher. "Not for two bits."

Eddie was looking proud enough to burst. "The

lady says she'll pay a dollar," said Eddie, waving a dollar bill.

"Oh, boy! Oh, boy!" cried Billy. "Bring him right in."

All the boys crowded around to pat the Saint Bernard dog. He was as good as gold. He stood still while Billy washed his big head and Rudy washed his back. Joe worked on his back legs and Kenny washed his front legs. It was a big job, but when the boys had finished, the Saint Bernard looked beautiful with his shining white and gold coat.

When Eddie and the dog departed, Billy said, "Oh, boy! Just one more dog and we can quit."

"Yeh!" said Rudy. "But we haven't any football." And when he said this the team looked very sad.

"Oh, well! Maybe we can wash more dogs next week and buy a football," said Billy.

Just then Betsy appeared. "Hello!" she said. "What are you doing?"

"We're in business," said Rudy. "We wash dogs. Only twenty-five cents."

"Yes," said Billy. "Just one more dog and we have enough money to pay my daddy for the soap."

"But we have to wash more next Saturday,"

sighed Rudy, "to earn money to buy a football."

"Oh!" said Betsy. "That's too bad." And she trotted off.

The boys sat down to rest.

Just as the Wilson twins were about to set off to find the last dog, Betsy appeared. She had Thumpy on a leash. "Here you are," she said. "It smells awful but you can wash him."

The boys just stared, but not at Thumpy. They were staring at the object under Betsy's arm. They couldn't believe their eyes. For under Betsy's arm was a football! She held it out to them. "Would you like to play with my football?" she said.

"Oh, Betsy!" cried Billy. "Do you mean it? Is it a real football?"

"Sure," said Betsy.

"Wheee!" cried the team.

"What a pal! What a pal!" cried Rudy, patting Betsy on the back. "You're on the team, Betsy. You're on the team."

Then he turned to the boys. "Come on, fellas," he said, "give her a cheer."

And they all cried, "Rah! Betsy! Rah! Rah! Rah! Betsy!"

And Billy rubbed Surething Flea Soap on Thumpy.

7

Just-for-Instance Presents

The football team had a wonderful time playing with Betsy's football. Little Eddie turned out to be one of the best players. Betsy wasn't so very good, but the boys were patient and encouraging. After all, it was her ball. Then one day she tore a big three-cornered tear in one of her best school dresses and skinned the toes of her new shoes. When she returned home, Mother decided that Betsy had played enough football.

The following night Father came home with a package under his arm. Betsy ran to meet him. "What's in the package, Father?" said Betsy, full of curiosity.

"It's a present," said Father.

"For me?" said Betsy.

Father nodded.

"A just-for-instance present?" said Betsy, dancing up and down.

"Righto," said Father.

"Oh, Father!" cried Betsy. "I think just-for-instance presents are the nicest presents of all, because they are the surprisiest surprises. When it's my birthday or Christmas, I know that I'm going to get a present, so the only surprise is what the present is. But a just-for-instance present is two surprises. The present is a surprise and getting it is a surprise."

Mother, who had been listening, said, "Oh, Betsy, I know just what you mean, darling." And Father threw back his head and laughed.

Betsy untied the package. She wondered why knots were always tighter on surprises. Things you didn't care about always fell open. At last the string was off. Betsy felt the weight of the package as she removed the wrapping paper.

When she lifted the lid of the box, there, to her delight, was a pair of shiny ice skates fastened to beautiful snow-white boots.

"Oh, Father!" cried Betsy. "Skates! Am I going to learn to skate at the rink?"

"That's right," said Father.

"How wonderful!" exclaimed Betsy, as she pulled off her oxfords and tried on her boots. "When may I go skating?"

"Mother has arranged for you to have a lesson tomorrow afternoon, at four o'clock," said Father.

"Well-l-l-l," said Betsy, "that's just the time

for our football game with the Screech Owls. The Screech Owls are another team in our school. Of course, I suppose they could put someone in my place."

"No doubt," said Father.

Betsy took off her skates and put her oxfords on again. She looked at the clock. "I'll just have time to run over to Billy's house before dinner. I want to tell him that I won't be able to play football tomorrow because I'm going to have a skating lesson."

Betsy opened the front door. Then she closed it again. She looked at the football that Mr. Kilpatrick had given her. She picked it up and tucked it under her arm. Father was sitting by the fire, reading his paper. Betsy went to him and he looked up at her.

"Well, little one?" he said.

"I'm going to take Billy a just-for-instance present," said Betsy.

"That's great!" said Father.

Betsy ran over to Billy's house. When she arrived, Billy was working on a model airplane.

"Hi, Betsy!" he said. "What do you know?"

Betsy held out the football. "It's a present," said Betsy.

"What do you mean?" asked Billy.

"It's a present for you," said Betsy. "A just-for-instance present."

"Golly!" cried Billy, his eyes popping. "You mean you're going to give me that swell football?"

"Yepper," replied Betsy.

"Oh, gee, Betsy!" said Billy. "That's swell. Thanks ever so much."

Then Betsy told Billy of how Mr. Kilpatrick had given her the football. When she finished, Billy said, "Do you know, Betsy, I think we ought to give Mr. Kilpatrick a present."

"Oh, I do too," said Betsy. "What shall we get for a present for Mr. Kilpatrick?"

"Well, I don't know," replied Billy. "We'll have to think about it."

"I have to go now," said Betsy. "I guess my dinner is ready. I'll see you tomorrow."

"Sure thing," said Billy.

When Betsy reached the door, she said, "Oh, I almost forgot! I can't play football tomorrow. I'm having a skating lesson. Father brought me a present tonight. Ice skates."

"Ice skates!" exclaimed Billy. "Boy! That's great! I'm going to ask for a pair for Christmas."

"Good-bye," said Betsy, as she went out of the door.

"So long," said Billy. "And thanks again for the football."

That night Betsy fell asleep thinking about the present for Mr. Kilpatrick.

The following day Billy came over to Betsy's house.

"Have you thought of a present for Mr. Kilpatrick?" asked Billy.

"No," replied Betsy. "I've thought and thought. I think it would be nice to go shopping for it. I like to go shopping. Then you see all kinds of things you never thought of."

"OK," said Billy. "How much money do you have?"

"I'll go see," replied Betsy.

Betsy went upstairs and got her pocketbook. She emptied out the money. It was all small change. When she counted it, it came to thirty-eight cents.

"I have thirty-eight cents," she said, when she came downstairs.

"I don't have that much now," said Billy. "But I will have it by Saturday. I can earn that much on Saturday morning, delivering grocery orders.

Then we can buy the present Saturday afternoon."

When Saturday afternoon arrived, Betsy and Billy walked into the shopping district of the town. They had seventy-five cents to spend on a just-for-instance present for Mr. Kilpatrick.

"There's no use going to the pet shop," said Billy, " 'cause we couldn't get anything there for seventy-five cents."

"Well, I don't think Mr. Kilpatrick would want any more pets," said Betsy. "The Queen of Sheba is enough."

By this time the children had reached a men's shop. Something pink in the window caught Betsy's eye. Pink was Betsy's favorite color.

"Let's look in this window," said Betsy.

The children pressed their noses against the glass.

"Oh," exclaimed Betsy, "look at that beautiful pink necktie." Betsy pointed to a pink satin bow resting in a box. "I think Mr. Kilpatrick would love that."

"What?" said Billy.

"That pink necktie," said Betsy. "I think he would just love that."

"Well, I don't," said Billy. "I think it's skunky,

if you know what I mean. I wouldn't wear it to collect garbage."

"It's beautiful," said Betsy.

"I won't put a cent to buy a skunky necktie like that," said Billy.

Then his eye lit upon something. It was a pair of bright red suspenders. "Now, there's something!" cried Billy, pointing to the suspenders. "There's something real!"

"What is it?" said Betsy.

"Those red suspenders," said Billy. "That's a present that Mr. Kilpatrick would like. They've got class."

"Yes," agreed Betsy. "They're awful nice."

"Nice!" cried Billy. "They're colossal!"

"OK," said Betsy. And the two children walked into the store.

They came out with the suspenders, neatly wrapped.

Billy's face was beaming, but Betsy looked longingly at the pink satin bow tie.

"How about it if I keep the suspenders until Monday?" asked Billy just before they parted.

"All right," replied Betsy.

Now that Betsy was alone she thought more and more about the pink necktie.

Finally she got her bank and opened it. Inside she found seventy-five cents. She put the money in her pocketbook and trotted back to the men's store. To her great delight the necktie was only seventy-five cents.

On Sunday she opened the package five or six times, just to look at the shiny pink satin bow.

When Betsy showed it to her father and mother, Mother said, "Do you think Mr. Kilpatrick will like a pink necktie, dear?"

And Father said, "Like it! Why, he'll be the hit of the police force in that tie."

The following morning Betsy stopped for Billy on the way to school. Billy had the box with the red suspenders under his arm, but Betsy had the box with the pink satin necktie in her coat pocket.

The children could hardly wait to see Mr. Kilpatrick, so they ran all the way.

When they reached Mr. Kilpatrick, he said, "Sure, and what's all the hurry this morning?"

"We have a present for you," cried Billy, handing the package to Mr. Kilpatrick.

"It's a just-for-instance present," said Betsy. And because Mr. Kilpatrick was Irish, he knew what a just-for-instance present is without being told.

"A just-for-instance present!" shouted Mr. Kilpatrick in his great big voice. "Sure, they're the best presents of all. Here! Wait until I open it."

The children watched the big policeman as he unwrapped the box. When he lifted the lid, he said, "My! Oh, my! Now did you ever see a more beautiful pair of suspenders! I always wanted a pair of red suspenders to match my red car. I can't thank you enough for such a present."

The children beamed with happiness. With each word that Mr. Kilpatrick spoke they felt more pleased.

Finally Betsy and Billy pranced off to school.

The other package stayed in Betsy's coat pocket all day. When school was over, Billy said, "So long, Betsy! I gotta run. We have a game on for this afternoon."

"So long!" replied Betsy and started off alone.

When she reached Mr. Kilpatrick, she said, "Mr. Kilpatrick, I have another present for you."

"Another present!" cried Mr. Kilpatrick.

"Yes," said Betsy. "It's just extra."

"Oh, Little Red Ribbons! You shouldn't have done all this," said Mr. Kilpatrick. "Two presents in one day!"

Mr. Kilpatrick unwrapped the box and took

off the lid. He picked up the pink satin bow. "Well! Well!" he said. "Now, isn't that magnificent! A magnificent necktie, I call that."

Betsy was so pleased she beamed. "I knew you would like it," she said as she started for home.

Several weeks later Father took Betsy and Billy to the movies. The two children were just settled in their seats when they spied Mr. and Mrs. Kilpatrick coming up the aisle.

"Hiya, Mr. Kilpatrick!" cried Billy.

"Hello, Mr. Kilpatrick!" said Betsy.

Mr. Kilpatrick waved his hand. Then he pushed his coat open. Then he put his thumbs under his red suspenders and winked at the children.

Mrs. Kilpatrick was all dressed up. She was wearing a pink satin bow in her hair.

8

The Christmas Fairies

Over the garden wall from Betsy's house was the house where the Jacksons lived. Mr. Jackson had married Betsy's first teacher, Miss Grey. Betsy and her little sister, Star, loved Mr. and Mrs. Jackson very much indeed. They spent many happy hours playing in the Jacksons' house.

Mrs. Jackson's maid, Clementine, had a little girl named Lillybell. Lillybell was three years old, and Betsy and Star were very fond of her.

Star played a great deal with Lillybell while Betsy was in school.

Lillybell and her mother lived in the apartment that Mr. Jackson had built for them, over his garage. Lillybell had her own bedroom and she had a playroom too. There Lillybell and Star played with their toys. Star could only say words, but Lillybell could say whole sentences and they understood each other perfectly.

About two weeks before Christmas, Mrs. Jackson told Betsy that she was planning to have a Christmas party.

"What kind of a Christmas party?" asked Betsy.

"Oh, I thought it might be nice to invite the fathers and mothers of the children who live around here. You children could have a Christmas play and we can serve sandwiches and cider."

"And doughnuts maybe?" asked Betsy.

"Oh, yes!" said Mrs. Jackson. "By all means."

"I think it sounds wonderful!" exclaimed Betsy. "I love having plays. What will the play be about?"

"Well, there is a very nice Christmas play," said Mrs. Jackson. "It is about a woodchopper and his wife who lived on the edge of the forest. The woodchopper was a very old man and he was very tired of chopping wood. One day he said to his wife, 'Oh, dear! I wish I had an ax that would chop the wood all by itself.'

"And his wife said, 'Perhaps the Christmas fairies will bring you such an ax.'

" 'Do you think they would?' asked the wood-chopper.

" 'If you believe it is possible, they will,' said his wife.

"Well," continued Mrs. Jackson, "when the woodchopper saw his friends, he told them about the ax that he had asked the fairies to bring and all of his friends laughed at him and said it wasn't possible.

"Then the blacksmith spoke up and said, 'Look at me. I would like to have a hammer that would beat the iron without my having to lift it, but would I be so silly as to ask the Christmas fairies to bring one to me?'

"And all of the people except the woodchop-per laughed and said, 'No. The blacksmith wouldn't be so silly.'

"Then the cobbler spoke up and he said, 'Look at me. I would like to have some scissors that would cut the leather for the shoes, all by itself. But would I be so silly as to ask the Christmas fairies to bring me such scissors?' And all of the people except the woodchopper laughed and

shouted, 'No. You wouldn't be so silly. Only the woodchopper is silly.' "

"And then what?" asked Betsy, as Mrs. Jackson stopped for breath.

"Well, one after another spoke up and said what he would like to have, and the only one who didn't think it was silly was the woodchopper. Finally Christmas Eve arrived, and as the clock was striking the midnight hour the Christmas fairies arrived; and sure enough, they had with them the ax that the woodchopper had wished that he could have."

"Oh, Mrs. Jackson!" cried Betsy. "I think that

is a lovely play. Let's get everyone together and start rehearsing."

Mrs. Jackson laughed. "All right," she said. "Suppose you tell the boys and girls to come over tomorrow evening and we will decide who will play the parts."

The following day Betsy told Billy and Ellen about the Christmas party and the play that Mrs. Jackson was planning.

Of course they were delighted with the idea, and soon the news had spread among the boys and girls of the neighborhood. When they gathered at the Jacksons' house there were over a dozen boys and girls.

Mrs. Jackson read the play aloud. The next thing was to decide who was to play the parts. After a great deal of chatter, it was settled that Billy would be the woodchopper and Ellen would be his wife. Christopher was chosen to be the blacksmith and Kenny to be the cobbler. There were so many characters in the play that most of the children had parts. The rest were stage directors, lighting experts, scene painters, and curtain pullers.

It took the children a long time to decide about the fairies.

"They ought to be little," said Ellen.

The children all agreed that the fairies should be little, but no one in the group was little enough. At last Betsy said, "I know! Let's have Star and Lillybell for the fairies."

"Oh, yes! Let's!" said Ellen.

"I think that would be lovely," said Mrs. Jackson.

And so it was settled that Star and Lillybell would be the Christmas fairies.

Rudy Wilson was the biggest boy, so he was to be dressed as the ax and the little fairies were to bring him in on Christmas Eve.

The children met at Mrs. Jackson's house in the evenings and practiced the play. The Jacksons had a big living room, and a large doorway led from the living room into the dining room. There, in the doorway, Mr. Jackson built the stage. He and some of the children painted the scenery which divided the stage from the dining room.

Mrs. Jackson and Betsy's mother spent hours making the children's costumes. The fairies' dresses were a delight to the children. They were made of white gauze with shiny gold spangles sewed all over the skirts. There were white gauze wings that fastened to the little tots' shoulders. Lillybell and Star thought they were wonderful.

At last the night for the party arrived. The children reached Mrs. Jackson's house at seven o'clock. By the time their parents arrived at eight, the children were dressed in their costumes and everything was ready.

The guests were seated in the living room and all was quiet. Just as Richard was about to pull the curtain, Mrs. Jackson said, "Where are the fairies? Has anyone seen the fairies?"

All of the children began looking around for the fairies. They were nowhere in sight.

"See if they are out in the audience, Betsy," said Mrs. Jackson.

Betsy left her post as stage manager and went into the living room to look for the fairies.

"I don't see them anywhere," said Betsy, returning backstage.

"Well, run upstairs," said Mrs. Jackson. "Perhaps they are upstairs."

Betsy ran upstairs. She looked through the rooms on the second floor but there were no fairies. Then she went up to the third floor. Outside the bathroom door she found Clementine.

"Oh, Clementine!" said Betsy. "Do you know where the fairies are?"

"I know where they are, all right," said Clementine. "They locked themselves in the bath-room and they can't unlock the door."

"Oh, Clementine!" cried Betsy. "What shall we do? It's time for the play to begin."

Clementine leaned her head against the door. "Lillybell, honey," she called. "You turn the little knob for your Mommy. You reach up and turn the little knob."

There was only the sound of a bumping noise on the door.

"I don't know how she ever reached up that high to lock it," said Clementine. "That child must have grown tall without my noticing."

"Oh, Clementine! I'll go and get Mr. Jack-son," said Betsy. And Betsy rushed down the stairs.

In a few moments Mr. Jackson arrived.

"I've been coaxing them for fifteen minutes," said Clementine, "but nothing's happened yet."

"I'll see if I can take the door off," said Mr. Jackson.

Mr. Jackson examined the door. Then he said, "No use. The hinges are on the other side."

"Oh, dear! Oh, dear!" said Clementine. "What a night for this to happen."

Suddenly Lillybell began to cry, "Mommy! Mommy! Mommy!"

Then Star burst out. They cried so loudly that everyone downstairs heard them. Betsy's father and mother came up and they tried to quiet the fairies. But the fairies just howled.

"We'll have to get the ladder out of the garage," said Mr. Jackson. "Then I can climb up and get in the window."

Mr. Jackson and Betsy's father went down to the garage. They brought the ladder out and leaned it against the house beneath the bathroom window. The ladder was not nearly long enough.

"My goodness!" said Mr. Jackson. "We'll never get up with this ladder."

The fairies were screaming now and nearly all of the parents were either up in the third floor hall or outside, looking at the ladder that was too short.

"You will have to call up the fire department," said someone. "They will send the ladder truck over."

"Guess that is what we will have to do," said Mr. Jackson.

Mr. Jackson went to the telephone and called the fire department. He told them about the difficulty and the fire department said that they would be right over.

This was all very exciting and the children

put on their coats and gathered on the porch to watch for the fire engines.

Soon they heard the clang, clang, clang of the fire bell.

"Here they come! Here they come!" the children cried.

"Goodness gracious!" said Mr. Jackson. "They don't have to make all that racket just to bring a ladder, do they?"

Just then the big red hook and ladder swung around the corner. "Clang! Clang! Clang!" went the bell.

Billy was so excited he kept saying, "Oh, boy! Oh, boy!"

Then, to the amazement of everyone, before the hook and ladder stopped at the curb the big shiny engine truck careered around the corner and stopped by the fireplug. Sparks shot out of its smokestack, looking in the darkness like giant Fourth of July sparklers. Right behind it was the hose truck, clanging its bell for all it was worth.

"For mercy sake!" cried Betsy's father. "They've brought out the whole fire department."

Before Mr. Jackson could stop them, the firemen came running up the porch steps with the hose. The men looked surprised to see the children on the porch.

Mr. Jackson held up his bands. "Hold it, men!" he cried. "There isn't any fire. You must have misunderstood. We just called for a ladder. Two little girls have locked themselves in the bathroom on the third floor."

"Oh!" said one of the firemen. "We got the message wrong. We thought it was a fire."

The men took the hose back to the truck and some other firemen carried a ladder around to the back of the house. The children followed and watched with great interest as the ladder went up, up, and up, until it reached the bathroom window.

One of the firemen ran up the ladder very quickly. The children watched him as he raised the window and climbed through. Then he stuck his head out and shouted, "OK, I'll come down through the house."

The other men took the ladder away and the children returned to the house.

When the fireman who had rescued the fairies came out of the front door, he was carrying a big pitcher of hot cider. Mrs. Jackson followed with a plate piled high with doughnuts.

"Gather 'round, boys! Gather 'round!" the fireman called out to the other men.

All the men came running to the porch. They

sat down on the steps and drank the cider and ate the doughnuts.

"Nicest fire I've ever been to," said one of the men.

"Never had cider before," said another.

"No," said another fireman, "only plenty of water."

Meanwhile, inside the house the children were gathered in the dining room and the parents were settled again in the living room. Betsy stood behind the scenes holding tightly to the two fairies.

Mary Lou stepped before the curtain. She bowed. "Parents and friends," she said. "We are about to present for you a play. It is called 'The Fairies' Gift.' "

"Clang! Clang! Clang!" came from down the street. It was the fire engines, going home.

And from behind the curtain came the little voice of Lillybell. "Fire engines! Come all for Lillybell." Then the other wee fairy piped up. "Fi-gins, Betsy! Fi-gins!"

Betsy said, "Sh-h-h-h!"

And Richard pulled the curtain.

9

Betsy and Her Valentines

Ever since the day Rudy Wilson learned that Betsy had given her football to Billy, Rudy had felt hurt. After all, he thought, he was the one who had wanted the football the most. And hadn't he been the one who had made Betsy Grand Matron? And finally hadn't he put her on the team? "After all that," he grumbled to himself, "she went and gave that wonderful football to Puff Porter." Rudy felt that it wasn't fair at all. Betsy should have given the football to him.

Rudy never said anything to anyone about it but he nursed his hurt feelings. The more he thought about it the more he wanted to do something that would make him feel that he had gotten even with Betsy and Billy.

Meanwhile Betsy and Billy had no idea that Rudy felt badly about the football. He had been glad enough to play with it. He had come to their Christmas parties and Betsy and Billy looked upon Rudy as a good pal. But the football stuck in Rudy's thought as a splinter might have stuck in his finger.

Once when Betsy and Billy were playing in the schoolyard, Rudy ran up to Billy and pushed him into Betsy. He pushed him so hard that Billy knocked Betsy over. Billy was as mad as a hornet, but Betsy said she didn't think Rudy meant to do it but that he was certainly getting awfully rough.

As the weeks went by, the children's days were filled to the brim. Betsy skated every afternoon after school. She had already learned to make the figure eight and now she was learning to skate backwards.

Billy had received some track and several kits for a miniature railroad for Christmas. So he spent most of his spare time in the cellar play-room, laying track.

Little Eddie Wilson had collected three stray cats and was always running into seafood markets, asking for fish heads for his cats.

Ellen was taking drawing and painting lessons. As soon as school was out, she would dash home to smear paint on large sheets of paper with her fingers.

Soon it was February, and Betsy's father had to go away on a business trip and Mother went with him. Mrs. Beckett, who had been Betsy and Star's nurse when they were tiny babies, came to stay with the two little girls.

As Valentine's Day approached, the shop windows were filled with valentines. There were all kinds: big ones, little ones, comic ones, pretty ones. Some had surprises in them, such as lollipops, sticks of chewing gum, candy sticks, and gumdrops. Betsy selected some of these for her best friends. She picked out one with a big red lollipop for Ellen, and one with a row of gum babies for her sister, Star. For Eddie she chose one with cats made of real fur.

Betsy looked forward to Valentine's Day. It

was such fun and so exciting to find envelopes slipped under the front door. Sometimes the doorbell would ring and when Betsy opened the door, there on the step she would find a little package. But no one was ever there.

One year she had found a little package there tied up with red ribbon. When she looked up the street, she saw Billy running as fast as his legs would carry him. So Betsy knew, that time, that Billy had left the package. When she opened it, she found a beautiful white handkerchief with a red heart sewed in the corner. Across the heart, embroidered in white, was the name "Betsy."

When Betsy thanked Billy for the handkerchief, his face grew very red and he said, "Oh, golly-wops! How did you know?" He made believe he was cross about it but he really was very pleased.

Betsy decided that this year she would make Billy a penwiper. Mother had given her an old pair of long white kid gloves and she had a scrap of bright red leather that she had been saving to make a pair of shoes for her best doll. With a cardboard heart as a pattern, she cut as many white hearts as she could from the old gloves. Then, from her precious piece of red leather, she cut one heart which she placed on the top of the little pile of white hearts. She fastened them all together by sewing a red button right in the center of the red heart. She ran the thread through and through the layers of kid. Betsy was delighted with the results.

When Valentine's Day arrived, she woke up feeling very happy. She jumped out of bed and ran right down to the front door without stopping to put on her bathrobe. There were no white envelopes lying on the floor. She opened the door on a crack to see if there were any on the step, but there was nothing on the step but the milk and cream. She guessed it was too early, so she scampered upstairs and crawled back into bed. She pushed her cold feet down into the warm covers and felt as contented as a kitten.

Soon Mrs. Beckett called out, "Come on, Betsy. Time to get up. It's Valentine's Day."

"I know," said Betsy. "I've been awake for ages. But there aren't any valentines yet. I looked and I've been listening. I haven't heard a sound at the front door and I haven't heard anything drop through the letter slot."

Mrs. Beckett went downstairs. "Well, you're mistaken," she called back. "Here's a great big one lying right by the door."

"There is!" squealed Betsy. She jumped out of bed and ran downstairs.

Mrs. Beckett was holding a large envelope in her hand and smiling broadly.

Betsy took it with eyes that danced. "Now who do you suppose left that!" exclaimed Betsy. "And I didn't hear a thing!"

Betsy opened the envelope and drew out the valentine. It was a folding one that opened up with fancy cutout paper in bright red. There were fat little pink cherubs holding a big heart with "To My Valentine" in gold letters.

"Oh, Mrs. Beckett!" cried Betsy. "Look! Isn't it beautiful!"

"Very nice, very nice," said Mrs. Beckett. "Now you go and get dressed." Mrs. Beckett bustled out to the kitchen and began making hot cereal.

Betsy continued to examine the valentine. Then she looked carefully at the envelope. She didn't recognize the handwriting.

"Now who do you suppose that is from?" said Betsy, following Mrs. Beckett into the kitchen.

"Well," said Mrs. Beckett, "one thing is sure. It's from somebody who got up early and somebody who is dressed. And that's something you're not. Get along or you will be late for school."

Betsy walked back to the front door, still examining the envelope. When she reached the door, she looked at the letter slot. Her mind took a sudden jump just like a Mexican jumping bean. She held the big envelope against the slot. It was much too big to go through and it showed no sign of having been folded. Then Betsy got down on her hands and knees and tried to slip the envelope under the door. The weather stripping interfered. It would have been impossible for anyone to have slipped it under the door.

Mrs. Beckett stuck her head out of the kitchen door. She saw Betsy on her hands and knees by

the front door. "Betsy," she cried, "what are you doing? I told you to go up and get yourself into your clothes."

Betsy looked up with a puzzled expression. "Do you know what, Mrs. Beckett? There's a mystery about this valentine. This valentine didn't come through the slot and it wasn't poked under the door."

"Well, you saw me pick it up off the floor, didn't you?" said Mrs. Beckett, looking a little flustered.

Betsy sat back on her heels. Then she shook her finger at Mrs. Beckett. "Yes," she said, "and I know who put it there. It was you, Mrs. Beckett. It was you."

"Oh, go 'long with you," laughed Mrs. Beckett. "Get dressed."

Betsy jumped up. She ran to Mrs. Beckett and threw her arms around her. "Thank you, Mrs. Beckett. It's such a beautiful valentine." Then she dashed upstairs.

As Betsy washed and dressed, she sang. It was going to be such a happy day. It was fun to have Mrs. Beckett put the valentine by the door. But Mrs. Beckett hadn't fooled her. She was too smart for Mrs. Beckett.

Betsy had spent so much time over the valentine that she had to rush around very fast in order not to be late for school. At last, she was ready. She snatched up her schoolbag and dashed out of the house. She had to run most of the way to school. She didn't have time to deliver any of the valentines that she had in her schoolbag. She would have to deliver them on her way home.

Just before she reached the school she passed Rudy Wilson. He was carrying a box under his arm. It was wrapped in white paper and looked just like a box of candy.

"Hello, Rudy!" Betsy said.

" 'Lo!" replied Rudy.

"It's fun, isn't it?" said Betsy.

"What's fun?" said Rudy.

"Valentine's Day," said Betsy.

"Well, you're not my Valentine," said Rudy.

Betsy looked a little surprised and then she shrugged her shoulders. "Well, you're not mine either," she said.

"You bet I'm not," said Rudy. "Billy Porter's your Valentine."

As Betsy hurried along by herself, she couldn't help wondering about the box Rudy was carrying. Who was Rudy's Valentine?

10

A Strange Valentine

The children couldn't keep their thoughts on their lessons, but they had a wonderful day. At recess and lunch time they slipped valentines into each other's desks. Betsy delivered some of hers this way, but the ones for her own neighborhood she saved to slip into letter slots or under doors, which was always more exciting.

To Betsy's great surprise, she found that she

had forgotten to put Billy's penwiper into her schoolbag. She remembered now that she had left it on her desk. Many of the children had little packages. Once when Ellen opened her schoolbag Betsy noticed that Ellen had a little package wrapped in bright red paper. Betsy couldn't help wondering whom it was for.

On her way home from school Betsy delivered all of her valentines except Billy's. She would have to go home and get his.

A short way from home she turned a corner and saw Billy ahead of her. He was scurrying along in the direction of her house, carrying a package wrapped up in white paper. It was evidently a box of candy. In his other hand, dangling from one finger, was a little red box.

Ha, ha! thought Betsy. *I know who gave him that. It was Ellen, 'cause I saw it in Ellen's bag.*

Betsy was sure that Billy was on the way to her house to leave the box of candy, so she walked very slowly. She didn't want to catch him leaving the package on the step. She must let him think she was surprised. Betsy stopped to play with a dog so that Billy would have plenty of time to get away.

Finally she decided that it was safe to go home. As she turned the last corner, she ran plump into Ellen. Ellen laughed and said, "Oh, Betsy! You scared me!"

Betsy laughed and said, "Oh, hello, Ellen!" And Betsy knew, and Ellen knew that Betsy knew, that she had been leaving a valentine at Betsy's house. But, of course, they both made believe that they didn't know.

"Well, good-bye," said Ellen.

"Good-bye," said Betsy. "I hope you get a lot of valentines."

"Oh, yes," said Ellen. "I hope you do too."

Just as the little girls parted, Betsy saw Rudy dart out from behind some bushes. *Now what has he been up to?* thought Betsy.

Billy was nowhere in sight, so Betsy ran down the street as fast as she could go. Sure enough, there on the step sat a white box that Betsy was sure was candy, and a little package wrapped in red paper.

Betsy picked them up and opened the door. Inside the floor was strewn with white envelopes. Most of them were for Betsy, although some were for Star.

She gathered them up and ran upstairs to her bedroom. She dropped the envelopes on her desk and sat down in her chair. She opened the red package first. She was sure that Ellen had left it for her. Inside there was a beautiful, little, fat, pink satin heart. It was a pincushion. Betsy placed it on her bureau. She stood back and admired it. She thought it looked beautiful.

Then she unwrapped the candy box. She lifted the lid while her mouth watered. What she saw made her scream. The candy box, instead of being filled with luscious chocolates, was filled with fish heads.

"Oh!" cried Betsy. "Oh!" She began to cry very hard. With tears streaming down her face she ran downstairs. She found Mrs. Beckett in the kitchen and she ran to her, holding out the dreadful box.

" 'Laws a mercy!" cried Mrs. Beckett. "What's that?"

Betsy was choking with sobs so that she couldn't speak. She put the box on the table, and with her arms across her eyes she cried as though her heart would break.

Mrs. Beckett put her arms around Betsy. "Oh, don't cry like that, darling," said Mrs. Beckett. "Tell me what it's all about. Tell me, dear."

Betsy just clung to Mrs. Beckett and sobbed. Mrs. Beckett patted her until the sobbing ceased.

"Now, tell me," said Mrs. Beckett.

Betsy felt exhausted but she managed to say, "It was Billy. He put that awful box of fish heads on the front step. And it was all wrapped up like a box of candy. I thought it was a box of candy."

"Billy?" cried Mrs. Beckett. "Billy Porter did that?"

"Yes," said Betsy. "I saw him carrying the box."

"Why, I never heard of anything so dreadful," said Mrs. Beckett. "He should have a good whipping. I suppose he thinks that kind of trick is funny. Well, I would like to funny him, all right. Don't you have anything more to do with that boy."

"Well, I'm glad I didn't give him that nice penwiper that I made for his valentine," said Betsy. "I'm glad I left it home this morning."

Mrs. Beckett carried the box outside and threw it into the garbage can. "If I catch sight of that Billy, I'll give him what's what," she muttered to herself.

Betsy's Valentine's Day that had started out so bright and shiny ended sadly. Even the valentines that she had picked up from inside the front door couldn't make her forget that terrible

box of fish heads. She told herself over and over that she would never, never forgive Billy.

The next morning when she woke she had a strange feeling that something was wrong. At first she didn't know what it was. Then she remembered. It was Billy. She was mad at Billy.

Instead of stopping for Billy, as she often did, Betsy went straight to school. When Billy arrived, he grinned at Betsy and said, "Hiya, Betsy! Did you get a lot of valentines? I know which one you sent me."

Betsy tossed her braids and said, "I didn't send you any valentine and don't you ever speak to me again."

Billy's face grew crimson and he said, "OK. If you feel that way about it."

At recess Betsy said to Ellen, "That was a lovely valentine you gave me. It's beautiful."

"I'm glad you like it," said Ellen. "How did you know which one was mine?"

Betsy giggled. "I saw it in your bag when you opened it yesterday."

Ellen looked puzzled. "But how could you tell?" she said.

"By the color," replied Betsy.

Ellen looked very blank.

"I have my pins in it," said Betsy.

"Your pins?" said Ellen.

Just then the bell rang and the children scampered back to their classrooms.

All of the rest of the month of February Betsy never spoke to Billy unless it was absolutely necessary in the classroom. She didn't go near his house and he didn't come to hers.

Betsy had never mentioned the terrible valentine box to anyone because Mrs. Beckett had told her not to speak of it. Several times Mrs. Porter had asked Billy why Betsy never came to the house, and Billy said, "I dunno."

Billy's birthday was the first of March and Mrs. Porter planned a birthday party for him. When he made out the list of friends he wanted to invite, Betsy's name was not on the list.

"Now, Billy," said his mother, "you must invite Betsy."

"I won't have her," said Billy.

"Billy," said Mrs. Porter, "this is all very silly. Betsy was one of your very best friends. She gave you that lovely football and now you don't want to invite her to your party. What is the matter with you?"

"Well, she didn't send me any valentine, and

she said she didn't want me to speak to her again," said Billy.

"Betsy said that!" exclaimed Mrs. Porter. "Why, that isn't like Betsy."

"Well, she did," said Billy.

"Then you must have done something to hurt her," said his mother.

"I didn't do a thing," said Billy. "I just gave her a valentine just like the one I gave Ellen."

"Then there has been some misunderstanding," said his mother.

"What do you mean, 'misunderstanding'?" asked Billy.

"Why, Betsy evidently feels that you have done something to hurt her," said Mrs. Porter. "The best way to show her that you wouldn't be unkind to her is to invite her to your party."

"Oh, all right," said Billy.

When Betsy received the invitation to the party, she threw it on her desk and said, "Humph! Billy Porter has invited me to his birthday party."

"Well, you'll not go there," said Mrs. Beckett.

"I should say not," said Betsy.

The following day Billy said, "Betsy, are you coming to my birthday party?"

And Betsy said, "I am not coming to your party."

Then Billy said, "Say, Betsy! What's the matter with you?"

"You know what you did," replied Betsy as she ran off to join a group of girls.

The very day of Billy's party Betsy's father and mother returned home. Betsy and Star were overjoyed to see them again. They both sat on Mother's bed, and Betsy chattered like a little magpie while Mother unpacked.

Finally Betsy said, "Billy Porter is having a birthday party this afternoon."

"He is?" said Mother. "Has Mrs. Beckett pressed your pink dress and did you buy a present for Billy?"

"I'm not going," said Betsy.

Mother turned away from the suitcase and looked at Betsy. "You're not going!" she exclaimed. "Why not?"

Then Betsy told Mother what had happened on Valentine's Day. Mother sat down on a chair and listened to every word. When Betsy finished, Mother said, "Why, darling, I don't believe it."

"But it's true, Mother," said Betsy.

"I don't believe Billy did it," said Mother. "It isn't like Billy to do a thing like that."

"Well, I know he did," said Betsy.

"No, Betsy, you don't know that he did it.

You just think he did it," said Mother. "What you know about Billy is that he has always been kind and loving and generous, and you have to judge people by what you know about them, not by what you think about them."

"Well, Mrs. Beckett said that I shouldn't have anything to do with him," said Betsy.

"But Mrs. Beckett doesn't know Billy," said Mother. "You and I do. Now take your pink dress down to Mrs. Beckett and ask her to press it."

Without a word Betsy went to her closet and took out her pink party dress. She carried it downstairs.

Betsy had just given the dress to Mrs. Beckett when the doorbell rang. Betsy opened the door and there stood little Eddie. He was carrying a bundle, wrapped in newspaper.

"Hello, Eddie!" said Betsy.

"Hello, Betsy!" said Eddie. "I came over to see if you have an empty candy box."

"I don't know, but I'll see," said Betsy.

"I'll tell you what I want it for," said Eddie. "But it's a secret. You mustn't tell."

Eddie began to giggle. "I'm going to play a joke on Billy," he said. "I've got some fish heads here and I'm going to put them in a candy box and wrap it all up to look like a present and give it to Billy. He'll think it's a birthday present. Rudy did it on Valentine's Day, only Rudy said his box was for a girl." Eddie laughed. "I'll bet she was surprised when she opened that box."

Betsy could hardly believe her ears. She stood as though glued to the spot. At last she found her voice and cried, "Eddie! Did Rudy do that?"

"Yes," said Eddie. "I saw him. And they were my cats' fish heads and I had to go ask the fish man for some more."

"Eddie," said Betsy, "that was a terrible thing for Rudy to do and you mustn't do it to Billy. That isn't at all funny. It's mean and cruel. You don't want to be mean and cruel, do you, Eddie?"

Eddie looked very solemn and his eyes were big and round. "Oh, no," he said.

"Well then, you take those awful fish heads home to the cats. Then come right back and we'll go out and buy Billy two nice birthday presents," said Betsy.

Eddie dashed off like a jackrabbit and Betsy went upstairs to tell Mother the surprising thing that she had learned from Eddie.

He was back in what seemed to be no time

at all, and the two children started for the shopping center of the town. When they returned, Eddie had bought a jigsaw puzzle and Betsy had bought an animal book for Billy's birthday present.

Betsy put on her pink dress and Mother drove the two children to Billy's house.

When Mrs. Porter opened the door, she said, "Why, Betsy! I'm so glad you came." Billy was right behind his mother and Mrs. Porter turned to him and said, "Billy, here are Betsy and Eddie."

Billy said, "Hello!" and took the two packages the children held out to him. He said, "Thanks a lot."

"Oh, Billy," said Betsy, "I'm so sorry I was mad at you. I thought you did something that you didn't do at all. I hope you will forgive me for being so horrid to you. Here's your valentine too."

Billy's face grew red and he scuffed his toe on the rug and said, "Oh, sure, sure. Thanks." Then he yelled, "Come on, everybody, we're going to play consequences."

Betsy's mother came for her when it was time to go home. When Betsy got into the car, Mother said, "Did you have a nice time, dear?"

"Oh, yes," replied Betsy. "I had a lovely time. You know, Mother, I felt just like me again and I haven't felt like me since Valentine's Day."

"I'm so glad," said Mother.

"It was silly of me to forget, all that time, what I really know about Billy, wasn't it?" said Betsy.

"Very silly, darling," replied Mother.

"Well, I'll try never to forget again," said Betsy.

CAROLYN HAYWOOD (1898–1990) was born in Philadelphia and began her career as an artist. She hoped to become a children's book illustrator, but at an editor's suggestion, she began writing stories about the everyday lives of children. The first of those, *"B" Is for Betsy*, was published in 1939, and more than fifty other books followed. One of America's most popular authors for children, Ms. Haywood used many of her own childhood experiences in her novels. "I write for children," she once explained, "because I feel that they need to know what is going on in their world and they can best understand it through stories."